football

Other Books in the Sports Heroes Series

football

Mark Littleton

Zonder**kidz**

Zonder**kidz**™

The children's group of Zondervan

www.zonderkidz.com

Sports Heroes: Football
Copyright 2002 by Mark Littleton

Requests for information should be addressed to:
Grand Rapids, Michigan 49530

ISBN: 0–310–70295-X

Editor: Barbara J. Scott
Art direction: Jody Langley
Cover design: Alan Close
Cover photography: Brian Bahr/Allsport
Interior design: Todd Sprague
Interior production: Beth Shagene
Interior Photography: Allsport

Printed in the United States of America

02 03 04 05 06 07 /❖DC/ 10 9 8 7 6 5 4 3 2 1

ACKNOWLEDGMENTS

Thanks to my editor Barbara Scott for her diligence, my publisher Gary Richardson for his willingness to step in and help when necessary, and to my family for not asking questions as I chugged through this project.

To the football players of the 1965–68
Cherry Hill High School West team.
I only watched and cheered from the stands,
but it was an amazing sight to see
you on that field.
Hope to connect with you all again some day.

CONTENTS

INTRODUCTION

Football is a contact sport. That means players come into contact with each other on the gridiron, sometimes brutally. I loved playing the game in backyards, on school fields, or anywhere, though never on a high school team. But I loved the tackling, the running with the ball, the long passes, the catch in the end zone.

Today, my football experiences are limited to television and in-stand spectating. I don't think I've actually thrown a football in several years. But I still remember the rough feel of the pigskin, the joy of creating a spiral that lands in a receiver's hands, the whump of one body into another in blocking and tackling.

You who read this book are probably more of a player than I ever will be. But then there's that song by Audio Adrenaline—"My Father's House"—that has the big backyard where "we can play football." Maybe we'll even play football in heaven. Who knows, maybe Jesus has quite an arm. Maybe Paul is one awesome middle linebacker. And Peter would have to be a lineman.

But wherever football ends up in the eternal perspective, for now it is a way to have good old American fun. I hope these stories will inspire you to engage in your sport of choice with even more exuberance and passion. Just remember, as Paul said, to "compete according to the rules." No holding. No face-masking. No delay of game, guys. Get to it!

1

TRENT DILFER:
Searching for Respect

Statistics	Born: March 13, 1972 Height: 6′4″ Weight: 229 lbs
Teams	Tampa Bay Buccaneers Baltimore Ravens Seattle Seahawks
Position	Quarterback
Honors	Seventy-game starting streak for Tampa Bay 11–1 in games he started for the Ravens Led Ravens to victory in Super Bowl XXXV

Photo by: Jed Jacobsohn/Allsport

Putting points up on the board is a quarter-back's job. But it's always nice to have a tough defensive team to stop your opponents from scoring too many points themselves.

In the 2000 season, the Ravens had both. With Trent Dilfer at QB, they racked up plenty of points, while holding opponents to less than 11 points a game on average for 16 regular-season games (165 total points).

Super Bowl XXXV proved to be the ultimate testing ground for the Ravens. Trent came through like the pro he is. Trent's Ravens faced the New York Giants, another defensive stalwart. The game evoked memories of great defenses of the past: the Steel Curtain (Pittsburgh Steelers 1974–79), the Lombardi Packers (Green Bay, late '60s and early '70s), Purple People Eaters (Minnesota Vikings, mid–70s), and Buddy Ryan's 46 defense (Chicago Bears, '80s).

Trent and the Raven offense found ways to move the ball against the Giant "D." Trent connected on

12 of 25 passes for 152 yards. With 6:57 on the clock in the first quarter, Trent delivered a perfect pass to wideout Brandon Stokeley. The ball whizzed into his hands at the ten and Stokeley dragged Giants' cornerback Jason Sehorn into the end zone for the Ravens' first score.

In the second quarter, Trent lofted another piece of spiraling sunshine to wideout Qadry Ismail as he sprinted down the sideline. That set up a field goal, which put the Ravens up 10–0 at halftime.

In the second half, the Ravens continued their dominance and ended up blowing out the formidable Giants, 34–10.

Early in his career, Trent didn't look like a future Super Bowl QB. He suffered through six stormy seasons in Tampa Bay, where he often argued with coach Tony Dungy about offensive strategy. The fans wanted him out of town so badly that they constantly booed him when he played. In the media, critics called for Trent to be traded.

Trent brought some of the heat on himself. He was outspoken, cocky, and sometimes downright arrogant. He admits to being rather immature early in his career. He says now, "I think many times you have to go through adversity and hard times for God to change your life. It took a lot of heartache for God to get through to me and to build those [positive] characteristics in my life."

Trent credits much of his development in character to the person he opposed so much in Tampa Bay: Tony Dungy, also a committed Christian. Dungy's display of calm under fire and grace in tough situations had an impact on Trent.

Trent first started seeking Christ when he was a college QB at Fresno State. Trent says he was pretty selfish back then, spending a lot of time after games drinking and chasing women. Trent recalls that in college he was "mean, cold, and selfish." His motto: "Anything for popularity." He attended church occasionally, but only because he thought it improved his image in the eyes of the public.

MARCH 31 1931

A Day in Football History

One of the greatest football coaches of all time dies in a plane crash. His name: Knute Rockne. During his thirteen seasons as head coach, he led Notre Dame to three national championships, had five undefeated regular seasons, and racked up the highest winning percentage in collegiate history — 881. Rockne was renowned for his halftime pep talks, including the classic "Win One for the Gipper" speech.

He would go to church Sunday morning and end up in a bar Sunday night. That pattern dominated his life until he attended an athletic camp. As he listened to a message at the camp, he realized that his attitude and actions were separating him from God. He realized that he needed to ask for forgiveness and become a real Christian.

Trent knew he was on the path to destruction. He needed a friend, a Savior, and a king who would be there always. He realized Jesus Christ was the answer. He invited Christ into his life.

That change provoked a powerful turnaround for Trent. He became committed right away, and his character improved one hundred percent. Trent says, "I spend a lot of my time on my knees, asking God to change me. Any time you ask God to change you, he will answer you, and it's often painful. It has been very difficult at times. The reward has been well worth the struggle, because as I see God change me I see him start to mold me into somebody he can use."

Trent's newfound maturity was evident by the time he signed with the Ravens. As he approached the Super Bowl, he humbled himself and talked to several champion quarterbacks about how to handle both the game itself, and the aftermath and the exhilaration—or disappointment—it might bring.

Great Gridiron Moments

In January 1987, John Elway took his team for a drive, in fact, for "The Drive." The Denver Broncos and the Cleveland Browns were battling for the AFC Championship. Six minutes remained on the clock as nearly 80,000 fans watched Cleveland appear to clinch the game, 20–13. Then Elway went into action.

He started on his two-yard line because of a botched kickoff return after a Cleveland TD. For the next three minutes, Elway scrambled and passed, getting the Broncos to the fifty-yard line.

But then the Dawg defense sacked Elway for an eight-yard loss. It looked like the drive was over, as Elway faced a third and eighteen situation. Dan Reeves, the Broncos' coach, called a time-out and told Elway to run a ten-yard pass over the middle. But Elway noted that the Browns' safety had been playing deep. He thought there might be a weakness there.

There was. He hit Mark Jackson at the Cleveland 28 for a first down. One minute, eighteen seconds to go.

Two more passes and the Broncos reached the Browns' five-yard line. On third down, Elway sent a screamer to Jackson in the end zone. Jackson pulled the ball in. Touchdown!

The late-game heroics sent the game into overtime. Feeding off the momentum of "The Drive," the Broncos kicked a thirty-three-yard field goal and went on to the Super Bowl.

Before he retired, Elway led the Broncos to two Super Bowl victories. But many football experts point to "The Drive" as the defining moment of his career.

After the game, Trent didn't try to capitalize on his fame. He wasn't featured in hosts of TV ads, but that was okay with him. He was serving God now.

One of Trent's most memorable moments was not in Super Bowl XXXV, but in their eleventh game of the season, against the Tennessee Titans. The Titans came into the game riding an eight-game winning streak and appeared to be bound for the Super Bowl.

Trent knew if the Ravens could upset favored Tennessee, they'd have a shot at the play-offs. So he went into the game with high hopes.

However, near the end of the contest, Trent made a bad decision and threw an interception. He expected fans to boo him, as they had done when he was at Tampa Bay. And he feared criticism from his teammates.

But when the Ravens got the ball back and Trent huddled with his ten teammates, they looked at him with hope and what he calls "belief." They believed Trent could pull it off and win this one. Trent says, "That was maybe the first time in my career, after making a mistake like that, that I returned to the huddle and saw ten guys looking back at me who probably had more confidence than I did. That singular moment has meant as much to me in my career as anything."

Interestingly, Trent didn't begin the 2000 season as the starting Ravens QB. He was backup behind Tony Banks. But eight weeks into the season, Banks had not been able to move the offense, and the coaching staff decided to give Trent a chance. Trent inherited an offense that hadn't scored a TD in sixteen quarters and forty-nine possessions. No team in recent history had such a dry spell since 1993, when the Indianapolis Colts played twenty quarters without getting the ball into the end zone. Trent knew it was time to put up or shut up, so he gave it his best.

Trent's best resulted in ten consecutive wins, an AFC conference title, and the world championship.

JUNE 8 1966

A Day in Football History

The National Football League agrees to merge with the American Football League (AFL). In 1970, the NFL would split the league into two conferences, the NFC and the AFC, with Pete Rozelle as the commissioner.

Trent says, "When I went to Baltimore, I learned that the process is as important as the game. I really learned to enjoy Monday through Saturday. I found a new love for the game. It's easy to say you love football when you're going to play it on Sundays. But when you're not and your whole week is about work and preparation, do you really love it? I found out that I did."

Rushing Records

Walter Payton is the NFL's all-time career rushing leader, rolling up 16,726 yards in his twelve-year career. In second place is Emmitt Smith, with 15,000+ yards — and counting — as of the 2001 season. During his career, Payton amassed ten 1,000-yard rushing seasons, an NFL record he shares with Smith and Barry Sanders.

Most Yards Gained, Season

2,105	Eric Dickerson, L.A. Rams, 1984
2,053	Barry Sanders, Detroit, 1997
2,008	Terrell Davis, Denver, 1998

Most Yards Gained, Game

278	Corey Dillon, Cincinnati vs. Denver, Oct. 22, 2000
275	Walter Payton, Chicago vs. Minnesota, Nov. 20, 1977

What does Trent have to say to young people who might like to someday stand where he has, looking over ten men on offense and facing eleven on defense, with more than a billion people watching—in the stadium and on worldwide TV?

The first thing, he advises, is to realize you'll be criticized. But you still have to play your best, even when people are against you.

That was one thing Trent learned in Tampa Bay. He didn't try to shield his kids from the criticism he received. He explained that bad things happen to you, and you must be courageous and always do the right thing. God, he told his kids, expects you to live a pure life no matter what happens around you. Even when fans and media call you a failure. Even when you're unfairly attacked and you want revenge.

Trent has discovered that, in the end, God is in charge of who achieves success. Success in his eyes is living obediently. And sometimes that obedience results in Super Bowl titles.

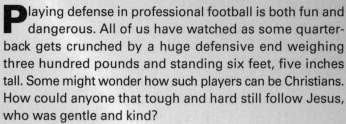

Hall of Fame Profile: Reggie White

Playing defense in professional football is both fun and dangerous. All of us have watched as some quarterback gets crunched by a huge defensive end weighing three hundred pounds and standing six feet, five inches tall. Some might wonder how such players can be Christians. How could anyone that tough and hard still follow Jesus, who was gentle and kind?

Strangely enough, the combination of gentleness, kindness, and goodness is not foreign to all defensive players. Consider the now-retired All-Pro Reggie White. Reggie, a defensive legend who led the NFL in sacks for two seasons straight (1987 and 1988), is an all-around tough guy. Ask a group of veteran offensive linemen about the toughest defender they ever faced, and the name Reggie White is sure to be mentioned. But he's also a Baptist minister. He preaches frequently in churches. And he loves to work with youth—teaching them football and the most important game of all, the game of life.

Reggie was raised by a single mom in Chattanooga, Tennessee. Reggie knew from an early age that he wanted to play pro football—on defense. When he watched great running backs on TV, he didn't want to be like them; he wanted to tackle them. To stop them cold in their tracks, to throw them to the turf and keep them from scoring. That's what thrilled young Reggie.

Reggie played football for his junior high team, then went on to excel in both football and basketball in high school. At six-five, he could slam-dunk a basketball with the best of them, but football was his first love.

Team Sack Stats

Most Sacks, Season

72   Chicago, 1984

Most Sacks, Game

12   Dallas, vs. Pittsburgh, Nov. 20, 1966
     St. Louis, vs. Baltimore, Oct. 26, 1980
     Chicago, vs. Detroit, Dec. 16, 1984
     Dallas, vs. Houston, Sept. 29, 1985

Reggie played for Chattanooga Howard High School, for coach Robert Pulliam. Reggie was good, but not tough. One day Pulliam took him aside and told him one day he could be a great defensive player. In fact, he said Reggie could possibly be the greatest defensive end ever to play football.

Then the coach began to push Reggie harder than he had ever been pushed in his life. And the pressure carried beyond the gridiron. One day, while playing basketball, Coach Pulliam was guarding Reggie very closely. The coach stood six-two and weighed about 280. As Reggie swiveled around him to make a shot, the coach threw his forearm up in the air and caught Reggie in the jaw. It felt as if his teeth were rammed straight into the back of his head.

Reggie wobbled off the court and into the locker room. There he sat on the floor and began to cry. A moment later, the coach stormed into the room. Reggie thought he meant to apologize. But the coach shouted, "If you think I'm going to apologize for busting you in the face, you can forget it." He added, "If you don't start getting tougher and begin dishing out what you have to, I'm going to keep knocking you around."

Reggie remembers, "Right then and there in that old, dingy, smelly locker room, I made a decision to be the toughest player around." The next time the coach decked him in a game, Reggie responded with his own brand of aggressive — yet respectful — play.

On the football field, Reggie played both offense and defense in high school, tight end and defensive end. He preferred defense, though. In fact, he almost hated offense.

As a senior, he was named Chattanooga player of the year. He also won "Two Sport Player of the Year" for his abilities in basketball and football. In winning this honor, he edged out future NBA star Patrick Ewing.

Reggie decided to stay in Knoxville, close to home, for college. He won a scholarship and planned to play defensive end for the Tennessee Volunteers, lining up against teams like Alabama, Auburn, Georgia, and Florida.

Reggie's toughness was soon challenged when he reported for practice at Neyland Stadium. One day he was blindsided by a huge linebacker. The player buried his helmet in Reggie's ribs. He was carried off the field on a stretcher, gasping for air.

He called his mom a few hours later. He said, "I'm going to give it up. I just can't take it anymore."

She responded, "Reggie, if that's what you want to do, then do it. But remember what you told me before you left for Knoxville."

He had told her that "as long as God had blessed him with the ability to play football, he would expend every ounce of energy in his body" doing just that — and he would never, ever give up.

His conscience stung, he reported for practice the next day. He decided to get tough and not give in. He began playing regularly his second game and didn't stop. He set his eyes on the Southeastern Conference Player of the Year award. No Tennessee player had won it since Tennessee coach Johnny Majors, back in 1956.

His junior year, Reggie suffered numerous injuries and missed a lot of playing time. Some in the press began saying Reggie was weak because of his religion. His Christianity kept him from being tough, they accused.

That made Reggie mad, and he decided his senior year would be his best — and most injury-free. He began working out with weights. Previously, he hadn't done much of that. He also ran on the track, building his cardiovascular system and muscle stamina. That year, Tennessee went from being last in the Southeastern Conference in defense to first.

At season's end, Reggie earned the honor he had been dreaming of: SEC Player of the Year. He was also a finalist for the Most Outstanding Lineman. He was selected for the Japan Bowl and Hula Bowl All-Star teams.

In 1983, Reggie was drafted by the Memphis Showboats of the fledgling USFL (United States Football League). He chose Memphis because it was close to home. He spent two excellent years with the Showboats, logging eleven sacks his first year and 12.5 the next. Then the USFL folded. In 1985, Reggie joined the Philadelphia Eagles, and he really began to bloom.

Reggie established himself as one of the NFL's best at getting to the quarterback. He also began ministries to young people, spoke in churches, and in general served his Lord with vigor.

2

PETER BOULWARE:
Sacking Them Hard

Statistics	Born: December 18, 1974 Height: 6'4" Weight: 255 lbs Wife: Kensy
Team	Baltimore Ravens
Position	Linebacker

Honors	1996: College football's defensive
	       player of the year for FSU
	1997: Rookie of the year in the NFL
	1999: Starter in the Pro Bowl
	1999: Teammates selected him for
	       the Ed Block Courage Award

Photo by: Doug Pensinger/Allsport

Like Trent Dilfer, Peter Boulware played in Super Bowl XXXV as a Baltimore Raven. But unlike Trent, the experience of jogging onto that field was a bit more emotional for him, owing to his explosive, excitable personality.

As he hurried onto the field for the big game, he thought, *Man, I am living a dream*. "As a kid," he explains, "you always dream of playing in this game, but you never really think you would get here. I looked around the stadium and realized I was living that dream. It was an awesome experience, the greatest you'll ever have as a football player."

Peter's immediate thanks that day were to God. He sees prayer and talking to his Lord as essential as breathing. He credits his success to God—and to prayer and hard work.

Peter's faith has deep roots. His parents are devout Christians. His father, Raleigh Sr., is an oncologist (a doctor who deals with cancer patients) at Richland Hospital in Columbia, South Carolina. His mother, Melva, works as a full-time homemaker and also owns a partnership in a furniture business. Peter's parents met at a Bible camp, fell in love, and married. When their children were old enough, they sent them to the same Bible camp.

Peter's brother Raleigh Jr. and sister, Kala, are also hard-driving, successful folks. Raleigh Jr. played defensive lineman for Georgia Tech's fine team in 1990. He works now as an engineer. Kala, a track and tennis star in college, is a medical resident at Vanderbilt University. Her husband is also a doctor. Looks as if Peter has nothing to worry about if he ever gets injured playing football. Michael, Peter's youngest brother, played linebacker at Florida State (Peter's alma mater).

SEPTEMBER
3
1895

A Day in Football History

The first pro football game is played, featuring two teams from Pennsylvania, Latrobe and Jeanette. Latrobe wins 12–0. The reason that this game is considered "professional?" Latrobe quarterback John Brallier is paid ten dollars for his efforts.

Peter's solid upbringing helps him face the temptations that come with being a high-profile professional athlete. At times he feels he is walking around with a sign proclaiming, "Hit me up for something; I'm an NFL star."

But Peter keeps his eyes solidly on Christ—and he hangs out with other Christians who keep him accountable. During his days at FSU, he roomed with Andre Wadsworth, who is now a star for Arizona. Andre taught Peter a lot about speaking in public, giving his testimony, and using his Bible as a basis for talks.

During his years at Florida State, Peter and Andre helped the team to a 43–5–2 record and a national championship. During his college career, Peter collected 32 sacks, from the defensive-end position. Despite his size, he was quick. He ran the 40-yard dash in 4.5 seconds and had a 37-inch vertical leap. And he bench-pressed 415 pounds. He was a dominating lineman in college, and scouts felt he would be a superb linebacker in the pros.

He came to Baltimore as a player accustomed to winning. Unfortunately, the Ravens weren't very good. In Peter's rookie season, 1997, the team finished 6–10. He had a great individual year, sacking opposing QBs 11.5 times and winning Defensive Rookie of the Year honors. He was also second team

Super Squads

Here's a look at teams who have made it to the Super Bowl. The teams are ranked by winning percentage.

Team	Wins	Losses	Winning Pct.
San Francisco 49ers	5	0	1.000
Chicago Bears	1	0	1.000
New York Jets	1	0	1.000
Baltimore Ravens	1	0	1.000
Pittsburgh Steelers	4	1	.800
Green Bay Packers	3	1	.750
Oak/LA Raiders	3	1	.750
NY Giants	2	1	.667
Dallas Cowboys	5	3	.625
Washington Redskins	3	2	.600
St. Louis Rams	1	1	.500
Baltimore Colts	1	1	.500
Kansas City Chiefs	1	1	.500
Miami Dolphins	2	3	.400
New England Patriots	1	2	.333
Denver Broncos	2	4	.333
Buffalo Bills	0	4	.000
Minnesota Vikings	0	4	.000
Cincinnati Bengals	0	2	.000
Philadelphia Eagles	0	1	.000
LA Rams	0	1	.000
San Diego Chargers	0	1	.000
Atlanta Falcons	0	1	.000
Tennessee Titans	0	1	.000

All-NFL. But Peter saw that this team needed an attitude adjustment. He recalls, "My attitude was that I was used to winning, and anything else was not acceptable. My mentality was we had to turn this thing around. We just had to do whatever it takes to win. I think that attitude kind of helped us turn it around."

But it was a slow turning. In 1998, the Ravens went 6–10 again. In 1999, they improved to 8–8, but they weren't regarded as one of the NFL's best teams. Individually, however, Peter continued to excel. He finished the '98 season with 83 tackles and 8.5 sacks. He was named to the Pro Bowl.

In the Ravens' 1999 mini-camp, Peter suffered a separated shoulder. An operation threatened to put him out for most of the season. His doctor said that he could play with the injury, then deal with it when the season was over. Peter wasn't sure what to do.

As usual, he went right to the Lord about it, and it seemed that the Lord gave him a green light to play. He was elated, but scared. He had to wear a harness on his shoulder, severely impairing his movements. In the end, he was a one-armed linebacker.

But the team decided that even with one arm out of commission, he was better than his backup. So Peter played. He rewarded his team's confidence by racking up ten sacks.

Great Gridiron Moments

It's Super Bowl XXII, January 31, 1988 — Redskins versus Broncos. Washington coach Joe Gibbs has an experienced quarterback in Jay Schroeder, but he opts to begin the game with backup Doug Williams, who becomes the first African-American quarterback in NFL history to be named starter for the Super Bowl. And in another bold move, Gibbs starts little-used Timmy Smith at running back.

The game starts badly for the Redskins. Williams seems to be suffering from the abscessed tooth he had removed the day before — during a five-hour procedure — and the Broncos seize an early 10–0 lead.

Gibbs sticks with his strategy. He keeps Williams and Smith in. In the second quarter, the decision begins to pay off. Williams hits Ricky Sanders for an eighty-yard touchdown toss. A few minutes later, Williams hits Gary Clark for another score, putting the Redskins ahead.

A bit later, Williams hands off to Smith, who breaks outside and dashes fifty-six yards for another TD. Then it's Williams to Sanders for a fourth TD — and Williams to Clint Didier for one more.

By the end of the first half, the Redskins have five touchdowns, including four TD passes in the second quarter alone!

Another touchdown in the second half puts the game out of reach for the Broncos. The Redskins win, 42–10. Williams earns the MVP award for 340 passing yards. On TV, he is asked what he's going to do next. He answers, "I'm going to Disney World!"

Joe Gibbs, who was questioned for his decisions to start Williams and Smith, is praised for his instincts and wisdom — and for sticking with his plans even when things weren't going well early in the game.

Peter's teammates were so impressed with his efforts that they awarded him the Ed Block Courage Award, given to the team's most courageous player.

Doctors operated on Peter's shoulder in the off-season. Soon he was well enough to play. He showed just how healthy was in an early-season game with Jacksonville, sacking the Jaguar QB twice.

At midseason, the Ravens were 5–3 and looking like play-off contenders. Trent Dilfer took over as starting QB, and with his leadership and a stout defense, the Ravens rolled toward the Super Bowl, losing only one regular-season game in the process.

SEPTEMBER 10 1992

A Day in Football History

Deion Sanders, a baseball player for the Atlanta Braves, signs a contract to play football for the Atlanta Falcons. (Three days later, he returns a kick-off ninety-nine yards for a touchdown.)

The Super Bowl was supposed to be a low-scoring defensive contest. It was, but only for the New York Giants, the Ravens' opponent. Dilfer and company put thirty-four points on the scoreboard, while the defense, led by Peter Boulware and Ray Lewis, shut down the Giants' offense. (In fact, the Giants' seven points came on a score by *their* defense.)

The future might hold more Super Bowls for Peter Boulware, a man firmly grounded in God's Word. He was disappointed when his friend Trent Dilfer left the Ravens for the Seattle Seahawks, but who knows? They might both play in the Super Bowl again—on different teams this time.

Hall of Fame Profile: Tom Landry (1924–2000)

Coaches come and go. Very few stay with one team for a long time—long enough to be part of a team's history, its identity. Tom Landry is one of those few. For twenty-eight years, he led the Dallas Cowboys, becoming a coaching legend in the process. Landry began coaching the Cowboys in 1960, the same year they entered the league, as the NFL's first expansion team. Landry had been a fine player, winning all-pro honors as a defensive back for the New York Giants in the 1950s.

But coaching was always his thing. He liked leadership. He liked devising defenses and offenses. Landry's offenses and defenses worked. The Cowboys became regular play-off contenders and earned the moniker "America's Team." Landry was named Coach of the Year in 1966 and 1975.

But the Cowboys didn't find immediate success. In their debut season, they went 0–11–1, the worst in NFL history at the time. But the team, under Landry's leadership, improved year by year. In 1965, the Cowboys posted their first non-losing record, finishing at 7–7.

At that time, Tom began thinking more about his faith in Christ. In 1959, he had been stopped on a Dallas street by a friend who invited him to a men's prayer breakfast. Tom didn't know how to turn him down, so he accepted even though he wasn't really interested. He was surprised when he walked into the Melrose Hotel dining room and saw about forty men eating breakfast and studying the Bible. They were going through Jesus' Sermon on the Mount. Tom had been in the middle of a personal struggle at that time over staying with the Giants or getting out of football altogether. Strangely enough, the Bible seemed to be providing answers to his questions about personal security and the future. He was intrigued and amazed.

Eventually, he became a Christian. There was no specific "born again" moment. But he slipped into faith as naturally as learning to throw a football or memorize plays. He realized that Christ had permanently changed his life. Suddenly, football was no longer number one in his mind; God was. Next family. Football ranked only third.

Thus it was during those early losing years with the Cowboys that Tom constantly turned in prayer to God for wisdom and insight. His most important decisions were made in his prayer room. He truly believed that Christ would be with him on the football field as much as in the church pew. Though he certainly wouldn't solicit God's help in winning games, he did seek wisdom about his management of players and his impact on their lives.

He also became a regular in speaking to youth, proclaiming his faith at Fellowship of Christian Athletes events. He got involved with the Billy Graham Evangelistic Association, speaking at crusades alongside the famed evangelist. Tom realized God had given him a unique position. He could have a tremendous spiritual impact on his players. He encouraged his men to attend football chapels and Bible studies. He was one of the first NFL coaches to be so bold about his faith.

Tom continued to lead the team until the 1988 season, when the Cowboys were bought by Jerry Jones. The new owner hired his friend Jimmy Johnson to take Tom's place as head coach.

It was a hard pill to swallow. But Tom had led the Cowboys for almost thirty years, the longest stint of any single coach with one team. He'd taken them from being losers to Super Bowl winners. He'd seen men come to Christ through his encouragement and leadership. And he'd shared his story with multitudes.

There used to be a sign in the Cowboys' locker room that revealed Tom's philosophy of life. It read: "The quality of a man's life is in direct proportion to his commitment to excellence."

Explaining his motto, Tom said, "What that means is that you have to get up each morning with a clear goal in mind, saying to yourself, 'Today I'm going to do my best in every area. I'm not going to take the easy way; I'm going to give 100 percent.'"

He was fond of quoting the apostle Paul: "Do you not know that in a race all the runners run, but only one gets the prize? Run in such a way as to get the prize. Everyone who competes in the games goes into strict training. They do it to get a crown that will not last; but we do it to get a crown that will last forever. Therefore I do not run like a man running aimlessly; I do not fight like a man beating the air. No, I beat my body and make it my slave so that after I have preached to others, I myself will not be disqualified for the prize" (1 Corinthians 9:24–27).

It's that kind of commitment that excels, pleases God, and often wins. It's the attitude Tom Landry had as a player, next as a coach, and finally as a spokesman for Christ. It's the attitude we should remember him for.

KURT WARNER:
Making a Difference for God

Statistics	Born: June 22, 1971 Height: 6′2″ Weight: 200 lbs Wife: Brenda Children: Zachary, Jesse, Kade
Team	St. Louis Rams
Position	Quarterback
Honors	1993: Gateway Conference Offensive Player of the Year for the University of Northern Iowa 1998: Holds NFL Europe record for passing yards, attempts, completions, and touchdowns 1999: MVP of Super Bowl XXXIV; set new record for passing yardage of 414 yards 1999: Played in Pro Bowl 1999: The Sporting News' NFL Player of the Year

Photo by: Brian Bahr/Allsport

Some say it was magic. Others claim it was a fluke. How could a man go from being out of football to leading a team to the Super Bowl and even being named the big game's Most Valuable Player?

Kurt Warner doesn't believe it was magic or a fluke. He credits his success to his relationship with Jesus Christ.

At one point, Kurt looked like a future NFL star. At Cedar Rapids Regis High School in Cedar Rapids, Iowa, Kurt became a star. His football coach needed a quarterback. All the players lined up to throw the ball. Kurt outdistanced all the others. So he became QB.

He did well in high school, then went on the University of Northern Iowa—where he rode the bench his first three years. He didn't play a single minute until his senior year. As a senior, he showed his stuff, winning the Gateway Conference Offensive Player of the Year in 1993. Kurt wanted to play in the NFL at that point, but his chances seemed small. Sure, he had turned in a fine senior season, but, at the same time, he wasn't good enough to start for his first three college seasons.

After graduating from college, Kurt tried out for the Green Bay Packers. He was cut during training camp.

What to do now?

Kurt didn't want to give up. He joined with the Iowa Barnstormers and played in the obscure American Football League from 1995–97. Even the top players in the league didn't get paid much. At one point, Kurt was so desperate for money that he took a job stocking groceries at a Hy-Vee—for $5.50 an hour!

Even at Hy-Vee, however, Kurt kept his football dream alive. When things were slow in the store, he

SEPTEMBER

17

1920

A Day in Football History

The American Professional Football Association forms with ten teams, including the Dayton Triangles, the Decatur Staleys, and the Canton Bulldogs. Each squad pays $100 to join the league. In 1922, the league will change its name to the National Football League (NFL).

Premier Passers

What quarterbacks have the highest passer ratings?

Highest Passer Rating, Career (1,500 attempts)

96.8   Steve Young, Tampa Bay, 1985–86;
        San Francisco, 1987–99
92.3   Joe Montana, San Francisco, 1979–90, 1992;
        Kansas City, 1993–94
86.4   Dan Marino, Miami, 1983–99

Highest Passer Rating, Season (Qualifiers)

112.8   Steve Young, San Francisco, 1994
112.4   Joe Montana, San Francisco, 1989

Most Passes Completed, Career

4,967   Dan Marino, Miami, 1983–99
4,123   John Elway, Denver, 1983–98
3,988   Warren Moon, Houston, 1984–93;
        Minnesota, 1994–96; Seattle,
        1997–98; Kansas City, 1999–2000

Most Passes Completed, Season

404   Warren Moon, Houston, 1991
400   Drew Bledsoe, New England, 1994
        Dan Marino, Miami, 1994

Most Passes Completed, Game

45   Drew Bledsoe, New England vs. Minnesota,
        Nov. 13, 1994 (OT)
42   Richard Todd, N.Y. Jets vs. San Francisco,
        Sept. 21, 1980

Vinny Testaverde, N.Y. Jets vs. Seattle,
Dec. 6, 1998
Warren Moon, Houston vs. Dallas,
Nov. 10, 1991 (OT)

Highest Completion Percentage, Career (1,500 attempts)

64.28   Steve Young, Tampa Bay, 1985–86;
       San Francisco, 1987–99 (4,149–2,667)
63.24   Joe Montana, San Francisco, 1979–90, 1992;
       Kansas City, 1993–94 (5,391–3,409)
61.83   Brad Johnson, Minnesota, 1994–98;
       Washington, 1999–2000 (1,821–1,126)

Highest Completion Percentage, Season (Qualifiers)

70.55   Ken Anderson, Cincinnati, 1982 (309–218)
70.33   Sammy Baugh, Washington, 1945 (182–128)
       Steve Young, San Francisco, 1994 (461–324)

tossed candy, Nerf balls, and even a real football in the store's aisles. Kurt feels that "training" taught him much about accuracy in throwing passes, both deep and short.

It was during this time that Kurt met Brenda, a divorcée with two children. The couple met in 1992 at a country-line-dancing party. Brenda soon began talking about faith and what it meant to follow Jesus. Kurt was interested. He was raised in the church and learned much about character and commitment from his parents. But Brenda brought something new to the table—accepting Jesus into your heart.

As their relationship grew stronger, Kurt reached a point where he knew he had to become committed to Christ. Then disaster struck. A tornado killed Brenda's parents. Brenda, devastated but strong in faith, impressed Kurt with her calm and her resilient spirit. Inspired by Brenda's faith, Kurt trusted Jesus and began attending St. Louis Family Church.

In time, he and Brenda married, and Kurt adopted her two children. One of Brenda's children, Zachary, had suffered brain damage from accidentally being dropped by his biological father. Doctors said Zachary would probably die. When Zachary didn't, they said he'd never walk, talk, or see.

None of it came true though, as God began to bless Kurt and Brenda for their faith and prayers.

In football, Kurt received an opportunity to play in NFL Europe for the Amsterdam Admirals. In Europe, teams play eight-on-eight, at indoor arenas created for basketball and hockey. The fast-paced, razzle-dazzle brand of play appealed to Kurt. He decided to go for it. He was a sensation—setting records in passing, attempts, completions, and touchdowns.

The Admirals were owned by the St. Louis Rams, and coach Dick Vermeil decided to give Kurt a look. So, after wrapping up the European season in

Great Gridiron Moments

A perfect season? Is it possible?

You bet. It was clinched in 1973 at Super Bowl VII, featuring the Miami Dolphins and the Washington Redskins. Miami had logged a perfect 14–0 regular season, but was considered beatable, even though their "No Name Defense" was intent on stifling the Redskins.

No one scored early, then Miami QB Bob Griese got his team moving. Mixing runs by Jim Kiick, Larry Csonka, and Eugene "Mercury" Morris with passes to wideout Paul Warfield, Griese guided the Dolphins to a 14–0 halftime lead.

The Redskins threatened to come back in the second half, when Miami Kicker Garo Yepremian tried to throw a pass on a broken play. The 'Skins' Mike Bass picked off the wobbly throw and sprinted forty-nine yards for a TD.

However, Miami's "No Name" defense stifled Washington all day, allowing no points against them. The game ended 14–7, Dolphins.

Miami finished the season undefeated, a feat no one has equaled since then.

June, Kurt headed for the Rams' 1998 summer training camp.

Kurt ended up being signed as a third-string quarterback. Trent Green was first string at the time and regarded as untouchable. Kurt didn't play at all till a late-season game that the Rams lost to San Francisco. He threw only eleven passes.

But Kurt's performance in practice—and in limited game action—made an impression on Vermeil. He moved Kurt to number two on the QB depth chart for the 1999 season.

Kurt's faith in Christ was growing quickly at that time. He recalls that the Lord "was a huge part of my success, that there's no way I could have gotten to the point where I'm at now without the Lord and his grace and his love. That's the underlying theme in everything I do. I try to let people know where I'm at, and what put me over the hump or made the biggest difference in my life, and that obviously was Jesus and my faith in God."

OCTOBER
3
1989

A Day in Football History

Art Shell becomes the first African-American NFL head coach—for the Oakland Raiders. (Shell formerly played for the Raiders, earning Hall of Fame honors for his fifteen stellar seasons as an offensive lineman.)

Just what happened in Kurt Warner's breakout 1999 season?

It was the dream season of all dream seasons for Kurt. First, Trent Green suffered a season-ending knee injury in an exhibition game. Kurt was sorry to see his teammate fall, but he savored the opportunity to prove himself as a starter. And he wanted to prove himself to Coach Vermeil, who gave him a chance to play in the NFL.

In the 1999 season, Kurt accounted for 4,353 total yards and forty-one touchdowns. The Rams ended the regular season 13–3, then won two play-off games to gain a berth in the Super Bowl.

Then came the give-me-a-miracle day at Super Bowl XXXIV, as St. Louis faced the Tennessee Titans. Kurt's arm was in great form as he threw for 414 yards, a Super Bowl record (although he also threw three interceptions). With only two minutes left in the game, the score stood at 16-all, with the Rams in possession of the ball at their own twenty-seven-yard line.

With the game on the line, Kurt hurled a perfect pass to Isaac Bruce. It turned into a seventy-three-yard touchdown play that sealed the world championship for the Rams.

Kurt received the Super Bowl MVP trophy—to complement his regular-season MVP honors. Kurt is one of only six players to pull off this impressive double award.

Play Like a Pro:
Tips from Kurt Warner

1. *Focus on the Catch.* Keeping your eye on the ball as you catch it seems easy, but it's not — especially when you know someone is ready to hit you immediately. As a receiver, extend your arms, lock the ball into your hands, then bring it into your body. Trying to catch the ball against your body will often result in it bouncing off your pads.

2. *Tackle Like a Truck.* You can't tackle what you can't see. Keep your head up and focus on the opponent's chest, not his legs. Drive your shoulders into the player, keep your head to the side of his body, and wrap him up firmly with your arms.

3 *Pass with Accuracy.* Practice, practice, practice. There is no substitute for practice. But make practice productive. Always concentrate on a target, whether it's throwing through a tire or at a spot on the wall. And never be satisfied. You must always believe you can do better.

4. *Follow the Coach.* Coaches want someone who will listen and respond to what they are saying. Sometimes you might think the coach is wrong, but if you get on your coach's bad side, you will pay the price. Always try to do the right thing immediately. Coaches love players who get it right after being told only once what to do.

5. *Have Fun.* A positive, fun-loving attitude is important. No one wants to be around someone who is negative. If you're not having fun, it might be time to find something else to do.

6. *Never Give Up.* Very few players are naturals at their sport. Many young players fall by the wayside because they believe they are not talented enough to play the game. Remember, there's more to success than raw athletic ability. You should always work to get better. Don't let failure get you down. Michael Jordan was cut from his high school basketball team. I didn't play in college until my senior season. Believe in yourself, but make others believe in you because of your tenacity.

—adapted from *Kurt Warner: The Quarterback*
by Howard Balzer

After his stunning Super Bowl season, Kurt was awarded a multi-million dollar contract with the Rams. He gave the first ten percent to his church. Church is a big part of Kurt's life. He also hosts a Bible study in his home. More and more players have shown up at the Bible study, which Kurt says allows him to minister to his team's spirit off the field as well as on it.

Despite all his success, Kurt still sees the success as just more to the glory of God. He says, "Although obviously [there have been] great blessings that the

Lord has given me, I'm here to make a difference for him. As long as I stay focused on that, I don't think I'll ever allow it to take away my humble attitude about it."

The 2000 season wasn't the best for Kurt. He suffered an injury to his hand in the early part of the season and was out most of the year. St. Louis didn't make it to the Super Bowl again, although they were a contender. As the 2001 season was drawing to a close, the Rams were once again in position to make a Super Bowl run. On February 3, 2002, although it was a close game, the New England Patriots beat the St. Louis Rams in the final moments of Super Bowl XXXVI by a score of 20-17.

Maybe there will never be another Cinderella season like 1999. Kurt says of that remarkable season, "It didn't just happen. It wasn't like everything has always been great. I've had some times where I had to struggle through some things, and I think now the Lord used that to keep me humble. I know it's not all roses. If you lose sight of what's more important, you can very easily be where I was five years ago and not where I am now.

"It's not just stepping on a football field, but it's how it affects people's lives for Jesus. I think that's what helps me stay grounded—that I know I'm here to do the Lord's work. I'm not here to make a lot of money or to get fame. Although there's obviously great blessings that the Lord has given me, I'm here to make a difference for him."

Kurt Warner is indeed making a difference.

Hall of Fame Profile: Mike Singletary

New Orleans, 1986. Super Bowl XX. New England Patriots versus Chicago Bears. Twenty-two men take the field. But one player has an edge on the rest. He's watched game films, lifted weights, eaten a high-protein diet, and drilled himself mentally and physically on all key facets of the game. He's linebacker Mike Singletary, whose pre-game preparation is second to no one's.

Mike, the defensive captain, has a great game, as the Bears crush the Pats. (Although he doesn't win the MVP Award, which he craved.)

The Sack Pack

Who has the most sacks in NFL history?

Most Sacks, Season

22.0	Mark Gastineau, N.Y. Jets, 1984
21.0	Reggie White, Philadelphia, 1987
	Chris Doleman, Minnesota, 1989
	Lawrence Taylor, N.Y. Giants, 1986

Most Sacks, Game

7.0   Derrick Thomas, Kansas City vs. Seattle,
            Nov. 11, 1990

6.0   Fred Dean, San Francisco vs. New Orleans,
            Nov. 13, 1983

            Derrick Thomas, Kansas City vs. Oakland,
            Sept. 6, 1998

            William Gay, Detroit vs. Tampa Bay, Sept. 4, 1983

Most Seasons with Ten or More Sacks

13   Bruce Smith, Buffalo, 1986–90, 1992–98;
            Washington, 2000

12   Reggie White, Philadelphia, 1985–92;
            Green Bay, 1993, 1995, 1997–98

            Kevin Greene, L.A. Rams, 1988–90, 1992;
               Pittsburgh, 1993–94; Carolina, 1996, 1998–99;
               San Francisco, 1997

During Mike's playing days, he ate, slept, and drank football. No one watched films longer or more intently. No one practiced longer. He was always the last one to leave the field. He was dedication personified. Some said he was as great as Dick Butkus, the Bears' powerhouse middle linebacker of the '60s and '70s.

As middle linebacker for the Chicago Bears in the 1980s and early '90s, Mike Singletary was known for two things: breaking offenses' spirits — and sometimes cracking his own helmet in the process.

He broke a few at Worthing High School in Houston, Texas, where, as a senior, he was ranked the third-best linebacker in the state.

He went on to Baylor University, where he cracked sixteen helmets in four years. Mike was one of those rare players who tackled with his helmet, not his shoulder pads. He smacked running backs like a battering ram.

He kept the broken helmets as trophies, lining them up in the equipment room. And he was so tough a player that he was willing to compete *without* a helmet. In a college game against Georgia, Mike lost his helmet during a play. But that didn't stop him from knocking over two blockers and then ramming headfirst into the ball carrier, taking him down. And he was only a sophomore! He was named Defensive Player of the Year in the Southwest Conference that season, setting a team record of 232 tackles in eleven games.

His senior year, Mike was conference Most Valuable Player, an All-America selection, and runner-up for Most Outstanding Defensive Player in all of college football. He averaged fifteen tackles a game, never had fewer than ten, and achieved thirty or more in three games.

The youngest in a family of ten children, Mike wasn't allowed to play football as a child. In fact, he spent much of his time in church. His father was a minister, and Mike was required to be in church for up to twelve hours on Sundays alone (He used to feign illness so he could go home and watch the Dallas Cowboys play on TV.)

His father finally relented about football, and Mike started playing in seventh grade. In his first game, his team was behind 25–0. Mike was a reserve linebacker with the nickname "Suitcase." He earned the nickname because he carried around a big black bag filled with notes on football plays and general strategy. In the fourth quarter, the coach finally called on Mike.

"Suitcase?"

"Yes, sir?"

"Get in there."

Mike eagerly took his place on the field. The opposition ran a trap play. Charging toward Mike came the largest human being he'd ever seen. Mike ducked and threw his hands in the air. The back rumbled over him and into the end zone.

Mike thought his career was over, but in reality it was just beginning.

Almost ten years later, Mike was a college star, a Heisman finalist, waiting to hear the results of the NFL draft. He expected to go in the first round.

But this was a draft filled with talented players: George Rogers, Lawrence Taylor, Freeman McNeil, and others. As team after team announced their first-round choices, Mike's name wasn't called.

Mike felt as if the world was caving in. He would never play, he thought. The teams were all against him. Someone up there had just said no!

Mike needed some air, so he left his hotel in Houston and began to pray: "Lord, only you know what's best. If you want me to play this game, give me a sign. The only team I want to play for is Chicago."

Less than a minute later, Mike heard someone calling him. It was his girlfriend, Kim, and her mother. "Mike," Kim shouted across the parking lot, "they just announced that Chicago has made some trade with San Francisco to move up in the draft. The Bears picked you in the second round."

Mike went on to have a brilliant career with the Bears, and perhaps the crown jewel was that Super Bowl victory against New England.

Sports Illustrated called the game a "vision of hell" for the Patriots. "It was near perfect, an exquisite mesh of talent and system, defensive football carried to its highest degree." At the end of the first half, the Patriots had *minus nineteen yards rushing.* Records were set. Most points scored in a Super Bowl. Greatest margin of victory (thirty-six points). Most sacks (seven). Fewest total rushing yards (seven). Mike even picked up a couple of fumbles.

But Mike Singletary was only one of many who performed with excellence that Sunday. His play inspired his defensive teammates, who banded together in the 46–10 rout. In this game, as all others, Mike "gave it all for the glory of God." And sometimes, one's "all" is enough to earn a world championship.

4

LUTHER ELLISS:
Crushing the Offense

Statistics	Born: March 22, 1973 Height: 6'5" Weight: 315 lbs Wife: Rebecca Children: Kaden, Olivia, Christian, Isaiah
Team	Detroit Lions
Position	Defensive tackle

Honors	1994: Consensus All-American
	     at University of Utah
	1998, 1999: Selected by teammates
	     to receive Mike Utley Award
	1998, 1999: Named to "All-Madden
	     Team" by legendary coach
	     John Madden
	1999: Pro Bowl selection

The QB calls the snap. "Hut-Hut!"

The ball is put in motion. Then, suddenly, a hulk of a defensive tackle flattens the two offensive linemen trying to block him.

He leaps over one body. Then a second.

The defender finds himself one-on-one with a blocking fullback, who blasts into his chest. The hulking giant throws him off.

No one left now but the quarterback.

Panicked, the QB tries to find a receiver downfield. He spots one. If only he can get the pass off in time . . .

Too late.

The hulk crashes in on him, blocking his vision. The QB curls his body around the ball, hoping to prevent a fumble.

A second later, he is forced to the ground.

Sack number one of the year for Luther Elliss.

Luther makes no bones about it. He loves to shed blockers, overpower fullbacks, and smother quarterbacks. At 315 pounds, six-foot-five inches of solid muscle, he's built to do the job. Guys who have been brought down by Luther Elliss remember the hit.

Who is this defensive force?

Luther Elliss was born in Mancos, Colorado, into a Christian family. Luther played basketball and football in high school. At his size, he stood out, especially at a school with only 120 students. But Luther had more than size; he had skill. He was All-League, All-Region, and All-State. He set records in football and basketball, which was then his first love.

As he looked forward to college, Luther wondered how he would do against bigger, faster

OCTOBER

2

1916

A Day in Football History

In the most lopsided victory in college football history, Georgia Tech wallops Cumberland College, 222–0.

competition. Some of his teachers and coaches encouraged him to try for a smaller college. Division One competition, they feared, might eat him up.

Luther looked at a number of schools. The one that offered him the chance to play both football and basketball, though, was the University of Utah. After high school, he headed west, realizing now that his body was best suited for the NFL, not the NBA. Playing professional football became his dream.

His freshman year, Luther did well on the grid-iron. He earned the Newcomer-of-the-Year Award. He made the All-WAC first team both his sophomore and junior years. As a senior, he was again All-WAC—and a consensus All-American.

Next, it was time for the NFL draft, and Luther looked like a prime pick. The Detroit Lions liked his potential. They selected him in the first round.

Suddenly a multi-million-dollar player, Luther quickly established roots as a defensive tackle for Detroit. He played every game his rookie year, building a reputation as a big, tough defensive stopper.

His second year, 1996, he recorded 6.5 sacks and the next year improved to 8.5 sacks.

Luther's sophomore season in the pros was significant for more than football. He had grown up hearing about Christ, and he often lectured about his faith and how his listeners should accept Christ. But

Great Gridiron Moments

It's 1991, Super Bowl XXV. New York Giants versus Buffalo Bills. Giants' starting QB, Phil Simms, is out with injuries, so backup Jeff Hostetler starts the big game.

The teams match field goals early in the first quarter. Then, late in the period, QB Jim Kelly marches the Bills downfield for a touchdown drive.

In the second quarter, the Bills get a two-point safety when Hostetler trips in the end zone and is sacked. But then Hostetler rebounds, driving his team eighty-seven yards to a TD. Score: 12–10, Bills.

In the third quarter, the Giants' defense holds the Bills silent, while the Giants' offense racks up another TD. It's 17–12, Giants.

Still another turnaround comes, though, when Thurman Thomas breaks free for a thirty-one-yard TD for the Bills, putting them on top again, 19–17.

The game is so tight that fans are on their feet for the whole final quarter, watching Hostetler engineer a drive that ends in a field goal, giving New York a 20–19 edge.

But Kelly answers the challenge. He moves the Bills to the Giants' 29. There, Scott Norwood attempts a forty-seven-yard field goal, only to have the ball drift to the right at the last second. No points.

The Giants take their second Super Bowl trophy home, and the city goes wild. Even without their starting QB, they win. And Hostetler shows what can happen when a second-string quarterback is mentally and physically prepared to become first-string.

Luther himself wasn't living what he was preaching. He says, "I was enjoying giving in to worldly things, telling God, 'I know I need you, but I only need you every once in a while. I don't need you all the time. I enjoy being part of this world. I'm not ready yet.'"

Luther's wife, Rebecca, had noticed the slide and was concerned. She joined forces with Lions' chapel leader Dave Wilson and a few close friends and sat Luther down. It was similar to the "intervention" some people do with alcoholic relatives, only Luther wasn't an alcoholic. He was a world-aholic.

It had to stop.

They read him the riot act, saying, "You're putting on this great facade, talking about Christ,

OCTOBER 12 1991

A Day in Football History

Quarterback Doug Flutie passes 582 yards for the British Columbia Lions of the Canadian Football League. He would go on to finish the season with 6,619 passing yards, the most in professional football history.

Trent Dilfer #8 of the Baltimore Ravens holds the Lombardi Trophy after the Super Bowl XXXV Game against the New York Giants at the Raymond James Stadium in Tampa, Florida. The Ravens defeated the Giants 34-7.

Defensive lineman Reggie White #92 of the Green Bay Packers leads a prayer group of Packers and Vikings at the close of the Packers 16-14 victory over the Minnesota Vikings at Lambeau Field in Green Bay, Wisconsin.

Photo by: Todd Rosenberg/Allsport

Peter Boulware #58 of the Baltimore Ravens celebrates on the field after the AFC Division Playoff Game against the Tennessee Titans at the Adelphia Coliseum in Nashville, Tennessee. The Ravens defeated the Titans 24-10.

Photo by: Andy Lyons/Allsport

Head coach Tom Landry
of the Dallas Cowboys
stands and watches from
the sideline during an
undated Cowboys game.
Photo by: Fred Vuich/Allsport

Head coach Joe Gibbs
of the Washington Red-
skins during a 20-7 win
over the Chicago Bears
at Soldier Field in Chic-
ago, Illinois.

Photo by:
Jonathan Daniel/Allsport

Kurt Warner #13 of the St. Louis Rams moves back to pass as he is rushed by Jevon Kearse #90 of the Tennessee Titans during the Super Bowl XXXIV Game at the Georgia Dome in Atlanta, Georgia. The Rams defeated the Titans 23-16.

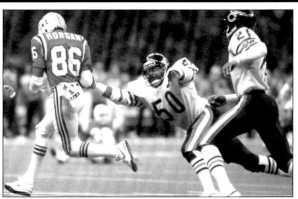

Linebacker Mike Singletary, center, of the Chicago Bears strips the ball from wide receiver Stanley Morgan of the New England Patriots during the Bears 44-10 win in Superbowl XX at the Superdome in New Orleans, Louisiana.

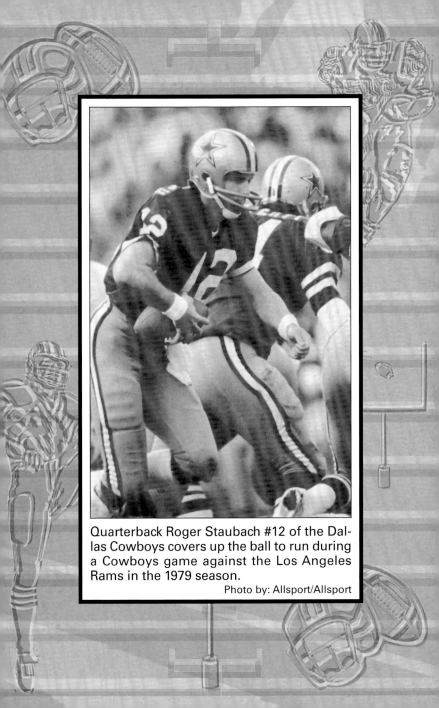

Quarterback Roger Staubach #12 of the Dallas Cowboys covers up the ball to run during a Cowboys game against the Los Angeles Rams in the 1979 season.

Photo by: Allsport/Allsport

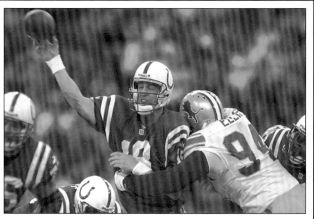

Quarterback Peyton Manning #18 of the Indianapolis Colts makes a pass under pressure by Luther Elliss #94 of the Detroit Lions at the RCA Dome in Indianapolis, Indiana.

Digital Photo by: Elsa/Allsport

A close-up of Tony Boselli #71 of the Jacksonville Jaguars as he smiles and looks on during the game against the Cleveland Browns at the Cleveland Stadium in Cleveland, Ohio. The Jaguars defeated the Browns 24-14.

Photo by: Jamie Squire/Allsport

Dennis Byrd #90 with wife acknowledges the crowd upon his return to the Meadowlands, the home of the New York Jets, following his recovery from a broken neck.

Photo by: Bill Hickey/Allsport

Photo by: Mike Powell/Allsport

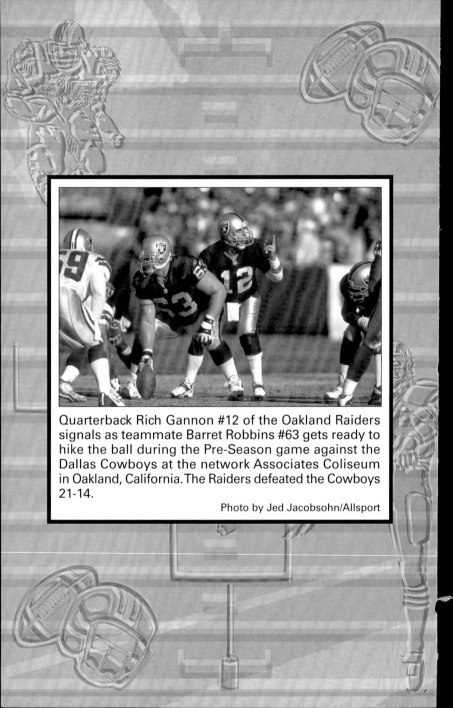

Quarterback Rich Gannon #12 of the Oakland Raiders signals as teammate Barret Robbins #63 gets ready to hike the ball during the Pre-Season game against the Dallas Cowboys at the network Associates Coliseum in Oakland, California. The Raiders defeated the Cowboys 21-14.

Photo by Jed Jacobsohn/Allsport

telling people what to do and how to come to know him, but you're not living it."

Wilson challenged Luther, saying, "Are you going to be a disciple of his or are you going to be part of this world? You've got to quit straddling the fence!"

It was a real pancake block on a defensive tackle! Luther got down on his knees and prayed. Then he stood up, ready to go all out for Jesus. He says now, "The hunger I have is for Christ. I'm hungry to know who he is. I want to know the Bible from Genesis to Revelation. I want to know the historical side, the background of the Bible. I want to know what the culture was like at that time. I want to know what God has in store for me—I just have this hunger to know.

"But then I want to share it. I'm at the point where I want to take it all in, and then just explode and share it with every person I come in contact with."

The result is that a new openness has come into Luther's life. He shares with his team members. He shares in public meetings. He shares every chance he gets. His teammates have noticed the change. James Jones, another Lions' lineman, says, "He's on fire for Christ. He's on fire for being a good husband, a good father, and a good person. He's hungry for success on and off the field. I know what he's striving for, and what he's trying to achieve as a player and as a person. When someone like Luther is playing for Christ, then you know he's going to give it his best shot. That's what you want from everyone, but you don't get it all the time. But when you have someone who is a follower of Jesus Christ, that's what he's going to give you."

Luther's first major challenge to his faith came in the summer of 1999. He broke the orbital bone (which holds the eye in place) under his left eye. He was body surfing in California at a place called "The Wedge." Six-foot waves made the afternoon a lot of fun until Luther decided to hitch a ride on one last big one and head home.

The biggest wave of the afternoon slammed him into the hard sand, knocking him out for a few seconds. When he came to, he was floating and couldn't feel anything. He thought he'd injured his neck, but it turned out to be his orbital bone.

Barely able to open his eye, he stumbled up the beach, his face bloody. He was taken to a hospital for treatment. For a while, he was seeing *triple*.

Luther arrived at the Lions' preseason camp ready to play, but still not completely healed. Because of his vision problem, he didn't know what to do except tackle the person in the middle of his vision. It was frustrating to go out on the field and never be sure whom he was up against.

His vision, though, gradually cleared. He performed so well in 1999 that he was voted to the Pro Bowl.

You can be sure Luther Elliss will be holding up his side of the line against ground and pass attacks. But more than that, he will hold up his side of the bargain in his relationship with Jesus. He'll be going all out for him, just as Christ went all out for Luther—and all of us—on the cross.

Hall of Fame Profile: Roger Staubach

While playing in the '70s for the Dallas Cowboys, Roger Staubach often found himself trying to overcome leads late in a game. In fact, he led the team to twenty-three fourth-quarter come-from-behind victories—including fourteen in the last two minutes or in overtime.

It's a remarkable record. Staubach was an exciting player to watch. You never knew how he'd come back, but somehow he'd find a way. Even though the Cowboys were a power team to be reckoned with in those days, they were often counted out as Super Bowl material. One year—1975—the Cowboys barely made a wild-card spot in the play-offs. They weren't expected to be championship contenders that year. But with Staubach in control, the team was always a contender. He could turn a game around — quickly.

Roger started football early, playing as a halfback and fullback in grade school. As a high school freshman, he decided to try out for the team at The Purcell School, an all-boys Catholic institution in Cincinnati. Roger found himself among more than a hundred other would-be players. He noticed that the shortest line was for ends. So he decided to be an end. He fared well, being voted "Best Leader" among the freshmen.

Because of his obvious leadership abilities, Roger was moved to quarterback for his sophomore season. Again, Roger made the team, but only as a reserve. As a junior, Roger was a starting defensive back, but only second-string at QB. He saw little action on the offensive side of the ball.

Finally, as a senior, Roger earned the starting QB spot. He liked the position. He enjoyed controlling the ball and running it sometimes, just as he did back in grade school.

More than forty colleges were so impressed with Roger's ability that they offered him scholarships. Roger longed to play for Notre Dame — a logical choice for a football star from a Catholic school. There was only one problem: Notre Dame wasn't one of the schools that offered him a scholarship. But he kept thinking of the Fighting Irish.

Gradually, Roger developed an interest in the Naval Academy. But that option presented another problem: His entrance exams in English were too low. What to do? The Academy suggested he go to a junior college.

So Roger headed for New Mexico Military Academy. Roger prayed hard about the decision and believes today the Lord sent him there.

According to the rules, Roger should have *never* been accepted to the Naval Academy. He was color blind. That was a strong enough handicap for disqualification. However, the Academy didn't discover this optical abnormality until Roger had passed his college boards and been accepted. Then it was too late to dismiss him. So the Navy kept Roger on board, warning him that he couldn't be a pilot or a member of the line crew on an aircraft carrier. That was fine with him. He was more interested in football than flying.

Roger played extremely well for Navy. During his junior year (1963), he won the Heisman Trophy, an honor rarely given to non-seniors. Navy had a tremendous season, posting a 10–2 record. A highlight of that year was the Army-Navy game. The game went to the fourth quarter looking like a blowout, with Navy leading 21–7. But then Army came alive. The Army quarterback led a drive and with six minutes to play, scored. The Black Knights ran in the two-point conversion and the Navy lead shrunk to 21–15. Another TD and extra point and Army could win.

It looked like Navy's rival would do just that. Army marched to the Navy seven-yard line with 1:27 left to play. The game was on the line — along with a trip to the Cotton Bowl. One minute later, Army faced a fourth-down situation, with no time-outs. With the crowd roaring, the Knights tried to call a play and run it.

Fortunately for Navy, time ran out before Army could snap the ball. The Midshipmen had won!

In the Cotton Bowl, Navy (ranked second in the nation) faced number-one-ranked Texas. It was no contest. Roger connected on twenty-one passes, but the Middies were outmatched against the powerful Longhorns.

Roger's senior year at Navy was anticlimactic. He was sidelined by various injuries, and Navy lost to Army — and didn't receive an invitation to a Bowl game.

However, NFL teams still liked the potential of Roger Staubach. Dallas drafted Roger, knowing full well that he owed the Navy four years of duty before he put on a football uniform. It was a risk, but it paid off, eventually.

During his time in the Navy, Roger did a tour of duty in Vietnam. He volunteered to go. He was a supply officer and saw no combat action, but the experience made an impact on him. He was struck by the poverty, pain, and suffering of the Vietnamese people, especially the children.

When Roger finally joined the Cowboys as a regular player in 1969, he was twenty-seven years old. He didn't win the starting QB job right away. Craig Morton was the Cowboys' starter, winning the position after the retirement of the great Don Meredith. Meredith had been with the team since its beginning, eventually turning a losing team into a winner.

In 1970, Cowboy coach Tom Landry divided regular-season playing time between Roger and Morton. But when Dallas went to the Super Bowl, against Baltimore, Craig started and Roger didn't play at all.

As the 1971 season began, Landry still hadn't made up his mind on a starting QB. Finally, with a third of the season gone, Landry settled on Roger. The scrambling ex-Navy man started the last nine games of the season. He led the NFL in passing completion percentage (60 percent), and averaged eight yards a carry as a rusher. The Cowboys finished 11–3 and fought their way to another Super Bowl.

That Super Bowl, against the Miami Dolphins, turned out to be a blast for Roger. He completed twelve of nineteen passes for 119 yards and two TDs. He threw just enough passes to complement the Dallas running game, which accounted for a record-setting 250 yards. Roger was voted MVP of the game, even though he didn't think he'd played that well.

Years later, Tom Landry would write of his admiration for Roger Staubach, who exemplified the never-say-die attitude of excellence that Landry cultivated in his players. "When I think of people I've seen in my career who embody this truth, I think of Roger Staubach," Landry said. "Twenty-three times he brought the Cowboys from behind to win—fourteen times in the last two minutes or in overtime.

"Roger's commitment to excellence improved the quality of his own life and the lives of everyone around him. During his career the Cowboys went to five Super Bowls. He started at quarterback in four of them, winning two championships. And in the two Super Bowls we lost, Roger was throwing the football into the end zone, giving us a chance to win, as time ran out."

What more can anyone say in tribute to a great athlete, a great Christian, and a great man?

5

TONY BOSELLI:
Holding the Line for God

Statistics	Born: April 17, 1972 Height: 6'7" Weight: 318 lbs Wife: Angi Children: Andrew, Adam
Team	Jacksonville Jaguars
Position	Offensive Tackle
Honors	1995: Named to Pro Football Writers of America All-Rookie Team 1996: Made *Sports Illustrated* All-Pro team 1997: Started in Pro Bowl 1998: Third Pro Bowl team in four seasons 1999: Fourth straight Pro Bowl

Photo by: Otto Greule/Allsport

The Jacksonville QB calls the play. "Hut-Hut-Hut!"

The center snaps the ball.

The ball is in the quarterback's hands. He drops back into the pocket as his offensive linemen battle the defense, keeping them away.

Anchoring the offensive line is Tony Boselli, who blocks with the best of them. Such defensive players as Bruce Smith know how awesome Tony is.

He pushes, he shoves, he clears paths for running backs. And when he protects for pass plays, he plants his feet and is practically immovable. He's like a 320-pound oak tree.

Tony keeps himself between a defensive tackle and the quarterback. No one is going to touch Mark Brunell, if Tony has something to say about it.

Whoosh!

The ball flies out of Brunell's hand, arcing downfield.

It flies into a receiver's waiting hands.

Tony's opponent stops, breathes hard, then looks at Tony. "You think you're pretty good, don't you?"

"You didn't touch Brunell, did you?" Tony asks.

That ends the conversation. Once again Tony Boselli has proven himself as one of the best—if not the very best—offensive tackles in the game. No one allows fewer QB sacks than Tony.

So, who is this offensive stalwart who hails from Boulder, Colorado?

As a kid, Tony loved any game featuring a ball. As a high school student in Boulder, he starred in football and basketball, being named to several state and national all-star teams.

NOVEMBER
2
1969

A Day in Football History

It's a battle in the air. Quarterbacks Bill Kilmer of the New Orleans Saints and Charlie Johnson of the St. Louis Cardinals each hurl six touchdown passes for their respective teams. The twelve touchdown passes set an NFL record. Oh, and the Saints win, 51–42.

From Boulder, Tony went on to the sunny skies of southern California, playing for USC. Tony played so well at USC that the Jacksonville Jaguars made him a first-round pick—a rarity for an offensive lineman. Usually, first-round picks are reserved for marquee positions, like quarterback, running back, linebacker, or wide receiver.

But Coach Tom Coughlin liked Tony. He met with Tony and his (then) fiancée Angi for over five hours one night over dinner. He put Tony through a workout and got to see his athleticism up close. At the end, he was sold. Tony Boselli would become the Jaguars' first pick and a key player for the first-year franchise.

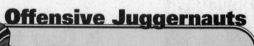

Offensive Juggernauts

Which teams have gained the most yards in a season, in a game?

Most Yards Gained, Season

7,075	St. Louis, 2000
6,936	Miami, 1984
6,800	San Francisco, 1998

Most Yards Gained, Game

735	Los Angeles vs. New York, Sept. 28, 1951
683	Pittsburgh vs. Chicago, Dec. 13, 1958

As a rookie, Tony didn't disappoint anyone. Although he dislocated his left kneecap in the pre-season and was out of action for four games, by the fifth game he was ready. He started the next twelve games, allowing only one sack. Reporters selected him for various NFL All-Rookie teams.

Then, in 1996, he started every game, giving up only three sacks. In a wild-card play-off battle against Buffalo, Tony cemented his reputation when he stopped the Defensive Player of the Year, Bruce Smith, in his tracks, allowing him only three tackles. That was when people began saying Tony ranked as the number-one offensive tackle in the league.

The event, though, that Tony credits with changing his life didn't happen on a football field. Instead, it was when he accepted Jesus as his Lord and Savior in 1995. After the whirlwind of being selected the first pick of the Jaguars (number two overall), graduating from USC, and marrying Angi, Tony began to sense that something was missing in his life. He arrived at the Jaguars' camp ready to do his best, and Angi soon built a friendship with QB Mark Brunell's wife. The two wives started a Bible study. One night Tony came to hear Greg Ball lead the study.

Greg preached about the grace of God and Lordship of Christ, painting an awesome picture of Jesus dying on the cross for our sins. When he asked the group if anyone wanted to accept Christ, Tony stood up. At the time, he admits he hardly knew what he was doing. He recalls, "I just knew something was missing, that I had tried to reach everything by myself, and that all the things the world had said were important, I already had. There was still something missing—something I was lacking—and that was to know the Creator.

"Unless you know the Creator, you don't know why you were put here, and you don't know your purpose here on this earth."

Although Tony had been raised in a church-going home and had heard about Jesus, he didn't know him personally.

Tony tries to read the Bible every day, even in the time-intensive schedule of a pro football player. "It's an everyday thing," he says. "I've got to wake up and say, 'Jesus, you're my Lord.' It's not a one-time prayer. I submit to [his] authority, and what [he] says goes."

How does this affect Tony in his walk with Christ? He says, "It's an encouragement to me to know that God is in control and that he has my best interests in mind. If I obey him and follow what his Word says, then my life will ultimately be fulfilled. When he created me, he had a plan."

That God is in control is evident in Tony's life as he has started several organizations that reach out to young people, helping them find their way in a tough world. It started the year he was drafted. He and Angi sponsored the Boselli Foundation, which encourages kids to become champions for God in their homes, at school, and on the playing field. Tony has also been featured in various public service broadcasts for the Ounce of Prevention Fund, Safe Harbor Boys Home, and the United Way.

The turning point came with the events at Columbine High School in 1999. (As a high school athlete, Tony had competed against Columbine, so the tragedy struck close to home.) He had started the "Victory Clubs" which give the truth about God, Christ, and the world to kids. He had started several in Tennessee and Louisiana. The clubs train young people to be bridge-builders, peacemakers, and leaders—to be strong in character.

Because of Columbine, Tony decided to bring the clubs close to his home in Jacksonville. The clubs are structured so that they support no particular religion while planting firm ideas about values and truth in the minds of kids. Tony says, "Even for people who don't know Christ, they should understand that there is a God, that he does have a plan for their life, that he is in control, and that he wants to see them fulfill their destiny."

Great Gridiron Moments

It was called the "Ice Bowl" for good reason; the field was almost a solid sheet of ice.

It was the 1967 NFL championship, the precursor of the Super Bowl. The Green Bay Packers faced the Dallas Cowboys. Tom Landry, Dallas's formidable coach, would square off against the winning-obsessed Vince Lombardi, whom some say is the greatest football coach ever.

The temperature was minus–thirteen degrees, and players felt the freeze, slipping and sliding all over the field. The Packers took the early lead with two touchdown passes. Dallas rallied before the end of the half, though, with a seven-yard fumble return for a TD, then a field goal. It was 14–10 at the half, Packers.

The third quarter was defense-dominated, with no scoring. In the fourth quarter, Cowboy halfback Dan Reeves thought up a play that just might work — a pitch from QB Don Meredith with Reeves faking a sweep and then throwing long to Lance Rentzel.

It worked. Rentzel scurried behind the Packers' defense, snagged the pass, and kept his balance on the icy surface all the way to the end zone.

Now it was up to Lombardi's Packers. They had four-and-a-half minutes to score and win.

Packer QB Bart Starr concentrated on short passes, throwing the Cowboy defenders off balance and onto the ice. The drive reached Dallas's three-yard line with less than a minute to play. Donny Anderson plunged three times across the scrimmage line, gaining on two yards. Facing a fourth-and-one, the Packers had to make a decision.

With the score 17–14, Dallas, Lombardi could go for an almost-certain field goal and tie the game. He could send it to overtime and take his chances. Or, he could go for the win right there.

In true Lombardi fashion, the Packers decided it was all or nothing, now or never.

Starr followed the block of Jerry Kramer and managed to wedge his way into the end zone. The Packers won the championship, 21–17.

Through the clubs, Tony hopes to make a lasting impact far beyond his life as a pro football player.

He also sees that everything good in his life right now is from God. "We have a great marriage," he says of his life with Angi and his two boys, Andrew and Adam, "but it's only because of what Jesus has done in our lives. I'd hate to see where our marriage would be without Christ. I always pray that I can be the dad these boys deserve—the dad God called me to be. I believe that it's a great responsibility. My sons are God's, and he's just making me responsible for their care. I just pray I don't mess up."

In the past two years, Tony has suffered some debilitating setbacks. Besides the dislocated kneecap before the 1995 season, in the 2000 play-offs, he suffered a torn knee ligament. That put him out for several months.

He recovered in time to get back into action in 2001. But in October, he suffered a torn labrum in his shoulder, which threatened to keep him on the sidelines for the entire 2001–2002 regular season and play-offs.

Whenever he returns to action, Tony says the injuries won't affect his aggressive, physical brand of play. He credits his Christian faith with keeping him on the cutting edge as an offensive tackle. In fact, he feels being a Christian has not reduced his aggressiveness, but made it stronger.

NOVEMBER 11 1990

A Day in Football History

Kansas City Chief Derrick Thomas sacks the Seattle Seahawks quarterback seven times, an NFL single-game record. (Incidentally, Thomas had QB Dave Krieg in his grasp for sack number eight, but Krieg wriggled free — and a game-winning TD pass.)

He says, "I think it's a stereotype that Christian men are soft. I think it's something that's really hurt the church, because that's not what God calls us to be at all. We're supposed to be mighty men of God. We're supposed to be leaders. We're supposed to be out there fighting for the kingdom of God and the name of Christ. That spirit and that attitude is how I approach the game. I'm going to play within the rules. I'm not going to try to hurt anyone on purpose or anything, but I'm going to play physical. I'm going to play hard. That's the way the game is played."

You can be sure Tony Boselli will be playing the game of life the same way, as he strives to be a good husband and father and bring glory to God's kingdom in the days ahead.

NFL Profile in Courage: Dennis Byrd

Dennis Byrd's second life began on November 29, 1992. To that date, he had been a professional football player — a defensive end for the New York Jets.

But his life changed in one day, in one moment. Late into the 1992 season, Dennis hadn't recorded a single quarterback sack, his worse drought in his four NFL seasons. He was a strong finisher, but the lack of sacks was getting to him. He began referring to himself as "His Royal Sacklessness."

On that day in late November, the Jets were playing the Kansas City Chiefs. Their quarterback, Dave Krieg, was a good scrambler, so the Jets needed to contain him, to pressure him into making mistakes.

Dennis, playing right end, was beating the Chiefs' right tackle, Rich Valerio. The defensive line coach, Greg Robinson, patted Dennis on the back and said, "Keep it up. You're gonna get there." Dennis could almost taste a sack. He wanted one, as long as it happened within the normal flow of the game. Dennis isn't the kind of guy who puts personal achievements ahead of the team.

Still, the "Royal Sacklessness" moniker was getting old. After all, Dennis had racked up seven sacks as a rookie, just one short of the NFL record for first-year players. And now, as a seasoned veteran, he had none.

The Chiefs opened the second half on offense, leading 6–0. On first down, Krieg threw a sideline pass and missed. Second and ten.

Dennis was sure the next play would be a pass. Everything connected — field position, the down, the yardage needed for a first. He figured Krieg would back up five to seven steps.

He got around Valerio and chased after Krieg, who must have sensed he was in trouble. He moved forward into the pocket to avoid the onrushing Jet. Dennis saw that he wasn't in position to tackle Krieg, but he leaped into the air and slapped at the ball, hoping he could at least force a fumble.

Just as his hand struck the ball, a figure came up into Dennis's field of vision. It was fellow Jet Scott Mersereau. They were going to collide.

Ordinarily, a football player, especially a pro, knows one thing about head contact: keep your head up. That way, the force of the impact is spread over the whole spine. When you put your head down, the force can be concentrated on a single vertebra, resulting in a break — meaning possible paralysis or even death.

But at that moment, hurtling through the air, Dennis didn't have time to think like a football player. It was all raw instinct. He ducked. He hunched his shoulders and tucked his head.

There was a terribly loud and horrid thump. Everything slowed down. Dennis hit the ground. It seemed as if everything stopped.

He lay there on the ground, on his back, trying to focus his eyes on the cool gray twilight. A few clouds floated by above him. The roar of the crowd seemed distant.

And then Dennis realized he didn't feel anything. His body stopped tingling, and he couldn't move. He tried to lift up his head. That was all he could lift. He felt a dry, crunching sensation in his neck. At that moment, he knew what had happened. He had broken his neck. His fifth cervical vertebra lay in chunks and splinters and specks inside his neck. One thought registered in his mind: *Don't move. Don't try to move anything.*

At first, the Jets didn't see Dennis's plight. It was Mersereau they were crowded around. Dennis had hit him in the chest and knocked the wind out of him. It was one of the hardest hits he'd ever sustained in professional football. He lay on the ground, trying to get his breath.

He lay there, waiting. Finally, Kyle Clifton, the Jets' middle linebacker, came over to him. "Let's go, buddy," he told Dennis. "Get up. Let's go." He fully expected Dennis to leap to his feet and get back into action.

But Dennis didn't move. He said, "Kyle, I can't. I'm paralyzed."

Kyle's face paled. He looked drained, fearful. He couldn't speak.

Next, Marvin Washington, another Jets' lineman, who was also Dennis's roommate, knelt by Dennis's head. "Dennis, what's the matter?"

"I don't have any feeling in my legs, Marvin. I can't feel my legs."

Marvin moved closer, whispered, almost hissed into Dennis's ear. "Just try, baby. Try." He turned away, pained, wiping a tear from his eye.

And suddenly, it seemed that everyone on the field grasped the severity of the situation. Pepper Burruss, one of the Jets' trainers, was at Dennis's head. He usually joked with the players. But now his voice was calm and measured. He said, "Hey, buddy. Just be still here. I got you. I'm gonna stabilize your neck."

In an instant, life changed for Dennis Byrd. He ceased being a professional football player. He became a quadriplegic, a man paralyzed from the neck down, and fighting the battle of his life.

But he wouldn't have to fight alone. Before a Jets-Bills game later in the season, there was a moment of silence for Dennis, followed by the national anthem. Overhead, a plane flew by with a banner saying, "GET WELL, DENNIS BYRD."

Before every game that Dennis played in the pros, he drew a little fish on the tape on his ankles. It was a pregame ritual. It was the same symbol the early Christians used to identify themselves as followers of Christ.

That Sunday, every one of the Jets wore the fish symbol on their helmets, with a little number 90 inside. Dennis's number. Even some of the Buffalo Bills wore the fish that day.

Into the fourth quarter, the Jets led 17–10. Then Buffalo's Jim Kelly began a drive that seemed destined to tie the game. Kelly lofted a pass to his wide receiver on the sideline. Brian Washington, the Jets' safety, cut it off, intercepted, and took the ball into the end zone for the final score.

As Dennis lay in a hospital bed watching the game on TV, he was astonished. He was dancing on the inside even if he could barely move. Then a camera zeroed in on Marvin Washington, Dennis's roommate his last three years in the pros. He stood in the end zone, jumping up and down. And waving his hand—with thumb, forefinger, and pinky extended. It means "I love you" in sign language. It was a symbol Dennis always waved to his wife,

Angela, as she watched him play from the stands. Dennis knew Marvin was signaling it to him.

That afternoon, four players flew out from Buffalo straight to New York City with a present for Dennis. They delivered it to his room. It was the game ball.

Dennis knew there was no giving up now.

He was soon transferred from Lenox Hill Hospital to a rehabilitation hospital called Mt. Sinai in New York, not far from Harlem. There, Dennis would spend the next few months getting himself back together.

It was a hard battle. When he arrived, he couldn't even sit up. Then he got feeling in his feet. Then feeling in his right side. Then movement. Two weeks later, the left side of his body began to respond.

He worked on everything: hands, feet, toes, thighs. He was moved into a wheelchair and learned to use the upper parts of his body to move it around. The therapists pushed Dennis, hard. They made him learn to eat by simply sticking a fork or spoon into a little glovelike cuff they put on his hand. There was progress.

And then one day in a therapy pool, Dennis stood.

With this breakthrough, he turned his attention to the next step, walking.

By the time the Super Bowl of 1993 came around, Dennis had walked. Walked!

On February 12, Dennis walked into a room on arm crutches and held a news conference. He was going home to Oklahoma, and he was walking — a man who had been a quadriplegic just weeks before. It was a miracle!

At the news conference, Dennis thanked the hundreds of people who had made it possible. He was so choked up that he could hardly utter their names. But he made it through. He concluded, "Four years ago, I came to New York a young Christian man."

Tears were close. He fought for breath.

"Now I go home a young Christian man and a New York Jet. I'm very proud to say that I'm a New York Jet."

The tears finally came.

". . . And I will be one forever."

Dennis went home to Owasso, Oklahoma. From that point, he continued to make hard-earned progress. He got his hands back, his feet. He could walk more efficiently. He could hold things. He could hug his wife and daughters.

The only thing he couldn't do was play pro football.

But maybe he'd done something far greater. He'd shown us that courage, commitment, and faith can overcome even the most frightful obstacles.

6

RICH GANNON:
Finally Getting to the Big Time

Statistics	Born: December 20, 1965 Height: 6'3" Weight: 210 lbs Wife: Shelley Children: Alexis and Danielle
Teams	New England Patriots, Minnesota Vikings, Washington Redskins, Kansas City Chiefs, Oakland Raiders
Position	Quarterback
Honors	1986: Yankee Conference Offensive Player of the Year for University of Delaware 1991: Set Minnesota record not throwing an interception in seven straight games 1992: September 27: for Vikings against Bengals, threw four touchdowns and had 147.8 quarterback rating, fourth best in NFL history; was NFC Player of the Week 1999: Named to Pro Bowl 2000: Pro Bowl starting quarterback 2000: MVP for the Raiders

Photo by: Donald Miralle/Allsport

Players call it being in "the zone." It's a difficult idea to pin down. For a quarterback, it means calling the right plays, avoiding the rush, and throwing perfect passes.

You step to the scrimmage line, needing three yards for a first down. You notice the defense is overeager. Two linebackers are going to blitz. Your blockers pick up the blitz and you hurl a pass downfield. Your tight end, who is normally covered by a linebacker, is wide open.

Touchdown.

The zone.

Rich Gannon was in the zone in 2000—for almost the whole season. After eight years as a backup QB, Rich finally emerged as a true leader.

Rich always knew he had talent, but he is a genuinely humble athlete who accepted his role as backup. In 1999, the role changed. Rich became starting quarterback for the Oakland Raiders. He had proven himself over many seasons as an excellent passer, play-caller, and scrambler. He could evade oncoming tacklers and throw on the run—or tuck the ball under his arm and sprint for a first down.

Rich was a natural as team leader. He felt great working with Jon Gruden, the young head coach who is only one year older than Rich. Jon had confidence in Rich, and it showed.

Rich showed athletic promise early in his life. He attended St. Cecelia's, a parochial school, and excelled at several sports, including football and crew.

His teachers remember him as a great kid whom everyone loved and who gave the love back. His high school coach's wife remembers Rich coming by on a date to give her a little present at Christmas.

JANUARY

31

1988

A Day in Football History

The Washington Redskins blow away Denver in Super Bowl XXII, exploding with five touchdowns in the second quarter. Final score: 42–10.

She says that kids just didn't do that kind of thing. But that was Rich—a kid who thought about others' feelings and needs.

After high school, Rich attended the University of Delaware, where he set twenty-one school records—in passing, rushing, touchdown passes, and just about everything else having to do with offensive productivity. It looked like he was on the way to a great NFL career.

Rich wasn't so sure. He made plans to go to law school in the event that the NFL draft didn't work out for him.

But the NFL draft did work out. Sort of.

Rich was taken in the fourth round, the 98th overall pick, by the New England Patriots in 1987. But the Patriots weren't even thinking of him as a QB. They thought they might turn him into a cornerback.

It didn't matter. Two weeks after taking Rich, New England traded him to the Minnesota Vikings.

It wasn't a great start in the NFL. Rich wondered why he was traded so quickly. But he didn't complain. He just decided to play his best and see what happened.

Unfortunately, Rich didn't get many chances to play his best. He backed up Wade Wilson and appeared in only four regular-season games. He threw a grand total of six passes.

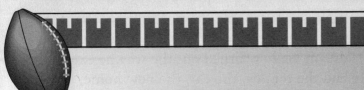

Prolific Passers

Most Yards Gained, Career

61,361 Dan Marino, Miami, 1983–99
51,475 John Elway, Denver, 1983–98
49,325 Warren Moon (various teams), 1984-2000

Most Seasons, 3,000 or More Yards Passing

13   Dan Marino, Miami, 1984–92, 1994–95, 1997–98
12   John Elway, Denver, 1985–91, 1993–97
9   Warren Moon, Houston, 1984, 1986, 1989-1991,
        1993; Minnesota, 1994-95; Seattle, 1997

Most Yards Gained, Season

5,084   Dan Marino, Miami, 1984
4,802   Dan Fouts, San Diego, 1981
4,746   Dan Marino, Miami, 1986

Most Yards Gained, Game

554   Norm Van Brocklin, Los Angeles vs. N.Y. Yanks,
        Sept. 28, 1951
527   Warren Moon, Houston vs. Kansas City,
        Dec. 16, 1990
522   Boomer Esiason, Arizona vs. Washington,
        Nov. 10, 1996

Rich started some hard thinking about his career. He realized the NFL, which had always been his dream, hadn't turned out the way he expected. He had the money, the car, the new home, but he knew something important was missing. He called it an "emptiness in his heart."

Growing up, Rich attended church every Sunday with his family, in which he was the fifth of six children. He says, "I felt like I was walking with the Lord and leading a life that was pleasing to him. But when I really sat down and thought about it, I realized that I wasn't, that I was a sinner."

Passing for Paydirt

Most Touchdown Passes, Career

420	Dan Marino, Miami, 1983–99
342	Fran Tarkenton, Minnesota, 1961–66, 1972–78; N.Y. Giants, 1967–71
300	John Elway, Denver, 1983–98

Most Touchdown Passes, Season

48	Dan Marino, Miami, 1984
44	Dan Marino, Miami, 1986
41	Kurt Warner, St. Louis, 1999

During his first season with Minnesota, Rich happened upon a chapel service. "I went to chapel, and I heard a speaker give his testimony," he recalls. "I felt so guilty inside because he had been wounded in Vietnam, and physically he was broken. He was missing an arm, a leg, and an eye. And here I was, a young, strapping male athlete who had basically everything. But I felt I wanted something he had. I knew what he had was that inner joy and peace that a relationship with Jesus brings."

Rich immediately talked with Tom Lamphere, the team chaplain. He left that talk with a solid understanding of the gospel. Later that week, he put his faith in Christ. His life immediately changed. He knew he was forgiven. He had inner peace, like the vet he'd heard that night in chapel.

It didn't change his situation in the NFL, though. He still didn't start. In his first three years in the NFL, he played in only seven games. During the 1989 season, he didn't play at all.

But God watches over his people. In 1990, Wilson left the Vikings, and Rich became starting QB. From 1990 to 1992, he led the Vikings in thirty-five games, appearing in six more as a backup. In a game against the Bengals, Rich threw for 318 yards and four touchdowns. His QB rating for that game was 147.8—the fourth highest in NFL history.

Great Gridiron Moments

Talk about comebacks — one of the greatest of all time happened in the NFC championship in 1981. The San Francisco 49ers faced the Dallas Cowboys. The 49ers had reached the play-offs for the first time in more than a decade. (In 1978 and 1979 they finished dead last in their division.) Meanwhile, Dallas had won two Super Bowls and missed post-season play only once in that same ten years.

Who would win? Everyone said Joe Montana and his 49ers didn't have a chance.

The game, though, surprised a lot of people.

The lead changed back and forth, until by the end of the fourth quarter, the Cowboys led 27–21. Montana, the 49ers' third-year QB, had five minutes to move his team eighty-nine yards. It was a long way to go, but Montana was a pure passer, and he thought he could make the drive with deft tosses, picking apart the Cowboys' defense.

He was right. With just over a minute remaining, the 49ers stood at the Cowboys' thirteen.

Montana's first-down pass, though, was incomplete. A run moved the ball to the six-yard-line, with fifty-eight seconds left.

Montana called for a corner end zone pass to Freddie Solomon. As the play unfolded, though, Solomon couldn't shake his defender.

Montana rolled out of the pocket, looking for Dwight Clark, his ever-ready receiver on the fly.

But as Montana scrambled, Huge Ed "Too Tall" Jones, Dallas's bone-crushing defensive end, closed in on him. He had to throw, even though Clark wasn't open.

As he fell backwards, Montana whipped a lob off the wrong foot. Many onlookers thought he was throwing the ball out of the end zone to avoid a sack.

But Clark, near the back of the end zone, leaped into the air and caught the ball on his fingertips.

Touchdown! The extra point made it 28–27, 49ers.

The defense held in the remaining seconds, and Montana's 49ers went to the Super Bowl — where they won.

Sometimes, when you toss up a desperation prayer, it gets answered.

But Rich's performance wasn't enough to make him the Vikings' franchise QB. Minnesota signed Warren Moon for the 1993 season and named him starter.

Rich, now a free agent, went to the Washington Redskins, who had become perennial Super Bowl contenders. Once again, Rich found himself a backup, holding a clipboard on the sideline during games. The 'Skins went 4–12, and management dumped all of its quarterbacks.

What would Rich do now?

Pray and pray. And hope he could find another team.

Rich's hopes dimmed, however, when he suffered a rotator cuff injury that required surgery to repair.

After the surgery, Rich went back to Minneapolis, which he still called home. He weighed his options. Tom Lamphere, still a mentor and friend, watched as Rich's faith pulled him through that tough year. Rich would pray, read the Word, and contemplate his future.

Rich says, "During that whole time, I never prayed to the Lord that he'd put me back in the National Football League. I never did that. I just prayed for guidance and strength—that he would take control of my life and my situation and whatever he had in store for us."

JANUARY 15 1967

A Day in Football History

Green Bay defeats the Kansas City Chiefs in the first Super Bowl (although the name of the game at the time was the less-impressive "NFL-AFL Championship").

Rich decided he couldn't sit by the phone, waiting for an NFL team to call, so he took an internship with a telecommunications company. In his off time, he worked on his arm, strengthening it and working on his passing skills. The 1994 season rolled around. Rich was ready to play, but no one called. Even as other quarterbacks were knocked out of action with injuries, no team saw Rich as a solution.

Rich and his wife, Shelley, continued to pray.

The 1994 season ended. Then, in March 1995, Rich finally got a call—from the Kansas City Chiefs. Rich was back in the NFL—but, once again, in a backup role.

Rich supported Steve Bono, waiting patiently for a chance to start again. But when the Chiefs named a new starter for the 1997 season, it was Elvis Grbac, not Rich Gannon.

The year 1997 was challenging in other ways too. Rich's baby daughter, Danielle, started waking up in the night, screaming and crying. She couldn't keep food in her stomach. She suffered daily bouts of vomiting and diarrhea.

Shelley took Danielle to several different doctors over a long period of time, but all of them said to let her cry through the night. It was just a typical colic problem.

Meanwhile, Danielle was starving, yet her belly bloated.

Finally, the Gannons took her to a specialist who, after numerous tests, told them their daughter had celiac sprue disease.

"What's that?" Rich and Shelley asked. They had never heard of the condition.

They learned that Danielle was unable to digest gluten. Gluten is a protein found in wheat, rye, barley, oats, and other grains.

Danielle was placed on a special diet. But it was tough finding foods that didn't contain gluten. Fortunately, through advice from friends and the Celiac Sprue Association, the Gannons were able to find stores that could fill their daughter's special needs.

Today, Rich is a national spokesperson for Celiac Research, which operates in conjunction with the University of Maryland School of Medicine.

With Danielle's problem under control, Rich turned his attention back to football.

Then, as fate would have it, Grbac was injured. Rich stepped into the starting role. He led the Chiefs to a 13–3 record. In 1998, he began the season as starter, passing for 2,300 yards in ten games. But late in the season, Grbac returned to action and reclaimed the number-one position.

Going into the 1999 season, it was apparent that Grbac was the Chiefs' man. Rich had a decision to make: Was he content to be a backup again, or should he try his luck with another team. He decided to head west, signing with the Oakland Raiders. Jeff George had been the Raider QB, but he was a free agent now, and there was a chance he might not re-sign with Oakland. He didn't, and Oakland coach Jon Gruden made Rich his number-one QB, including the play-calling responsibility. For the first time in his NFL career, Rich felt he was truly respected as a leader. It was a feeling he hadn't experienced since college.

He told reporters, "In order to play this position and to be successful, I think you need to know . . . that you are the guy; it's your offensive football team and that regardless of what happens, it is going to continue to be your football team."

The Raiders went 8–8 in 1999. Rich racked up 3,840 yards passing and an 86.5 QB rating that year. His twenty-four touchdown passes ranked fourth in the league. He was named to the Pro Bowl.

It looked like Rich was moving up.

Then came 2000. During the regular season, Rich completed sixty percent of his passes, connecting on 284 of 473, for 3,430 yards. He threw twenty-eight touchdown passes, while tossing only eleven interceptions. His QB rating skied to 98.4. What's more, he rushed for 529 yards, second best on the team. Best of all, the Raiders went 13–3.

They made it to the AFC championship game, where they lost to the eventual world champion Baltimore Ravens.

Rich continued his hot streak in 2001. As the regular season drew to a close, the Raiders led the AFC's Western Conference, and some media experts were calling Rich the best quarterback in football.

Rich says his faith is an important component of his hard-won success: "One thing I've noticed in my fourteen years is that the most disciplined, the most prepared, the most consistent guys you can count on in this business are Christians. That's not to say that other guys who aren't Christians aren't professional, but the guys who have a relationship with the Lord are able to set aside the distractions of everyday life, and they are able to focus and concentrate. They have their personal lives in order, so they can put all the nonsense aside and focus on their job."

This book is testimony to that fact. It features three Christian quarterbacks, including Hall of Famer Roger Staubach.

What is the key to their success?

It's not just football expertise and athletic talent. It's not just performance on the field. It's a commitment to the Lord that allows you to go for excellence and keep the devil and his tricks on the sideline.

With that kind of faith, who can lose?

Hall of Fame Profile:
Joe Gibbs

In many ways, coaching an NFL football team is harder than playing. Coaches shoulder most of the blame for losses, yet they often don't get credit for wins. And when you're a coach, everyone, from players to fans to media, second-guesses you.

Joe Gibbs, former head man for the Washington Redskins, knows all about these pressures. And he knows how hard it is to earn—and keep—a head-coaching job in the NFL. He was impressive as offensive coordinator for Don Coryell's San Diego Chargers. With Gibbs guiding the explosive "Air Coryell" offense, the Chargers were a hot team, even making it to the Super Bowl. Jack Kent Cooke, owner of the Washington Redskins, took note of Gibbs. He wanted to rebuild a winning team. He thought Gibbs could do it, and offered him the position of head coach.

Joe came to Washington full of hope and ambition. Being a head coach had been his life's dream. Now he was leader of a team with a rich football history. The list of previous Washington coaches was impressive: Ray Flaherty, George Allen, and even the legendary Vince Lombardi.

Only two years later, Gibbs' team found itself in the NFC championship game, against longtime rival the Dallas Cowboys. It was January 22, 1983, and the crowd noise filled the stadium like the roar of Niagara Falls. Fans screamed, "We want Dallas! We want Dallas!"

Dallas drew first blood with a field goal. Washington answered with two touchdowns—on a pass to Charlie Brown and then a John Riggins power-plunge. The Redskins went into the locker room at halftime ahead, 14–3.

In the third quarter, Washington added a touchdown, while the Cowboys chalked up two. It was 21–17, Redskins, going into the fourth.

The Redskins padded their lead with a Mark Moseley field goal. The 'Skins suddenly had a seven-point lead. An interception later in the final period sealed the victory. The Redskins were headed for the Super Bowl! Their opponent was the Miami Dolphins, Don Shula's juggernaut, who some considered the best team in football. Ever.

They met in Pasadena, California, on January 30. The Redskins entered the game looking for their first world championship in forty years.

Joe Gibbs admits to being a man of faith, but he doesn't usually just open his Bible and take what's there. He's more studious, looking for the passage that will meet a need.

But on Super Bowl morning, he opened the book to the story of David and Goliath. It seemed almost a sign, even though the coach knew God didn't choose sides in football games. But Joe took it as the assurance he needed that he was in the right place at the right time. Now it was up to his team.

It turned out to be an agonizing trial by fire for Joe and the Redskins.

Miami struck gold in the first quarter with a seventy-six-yard pass. 7–0. In the second quarter, Moseley booted a field goal for Washington, but then Miami's kicker, Uwe Von Schaman, added three points for the Dolphins.

Before the quarter ended, Joe Theismann capped an eighty-yard drive with the Redskins' first touchdown. It looked as if the half would end in a tie.

But with only two minutes remaining in the second quarter, Miami's Fulton Walker returned a kickoff ninety-eight yards for a score. Coach Gibbs was worried. The Dolphins now had the momentum.

In the third quarter, a Moseley field goal pulled the Redskins a bit closer.

Then, early in the fourth quarter, Joe faced one of those defining moments for coaches. The 'Skins had the ball on the Miami 43. They were too far away to attempt a field goal. They could punt and try to put Miami in bad field position. Or they could go for it. After all, they had John Riggins, perhaps the best fullback in the NFL. But if they didn't make a first down, Miami would have the ball in great field position.

After weighing his options, Coach Gibbs decided to go for it. And Riggins came through. He ran, dodged, pushed, and powered forty-three yards to the goal line. TD. 20–17, Redskins leading.

Late in the fourth quarter, the 'Skins would score again, and the game ended, 27–17. It was a classic hard-fought battle. Joe Gibbs, in only his second year as head coach, had won the big one.

When Joe thinks about that season and that game, he always goes back to that fourth and one. It was a huge risk, but when you make a courageous decision, the result can be a thing of beauty.

Today, Joe says, "I [have] realized that in life I'm always at fourth and one, and there are those who are urging me to go for it. Don't play safe, don't play the percentages. Go for it."

These days, Joe spends his time racing cars, playing racquetball, and enjoying his family. In faith he tries to make choices that will honor God, make his family secure, and be a Christian leader — worthy goals in the game of life.

REFERENCES

Bentz, Rob. "Surf and Turf," *Sports Spectrum* (November-December 2000): 21.

Branon, Dave, and Paul Johnson. "Out of Nowhere?" *Sports Spectrum* (January-February 2001): 27–29.

Byrd, Dennis, with Michael D'Orso. *Rise and Walk* (Grand Rapids, MI: Harper Collins/Zondervan, 1993), 2–3, 233.

Crosby, Jim. "Super Boulware," *Sports Spectrum* (September-October 2001): 18, 20, 288–89.

Gibbs, Joe, with Jerry Jenkins. *Fourth and One* (Nashville: Thomas Nelson, 1991), 150.

Robbins, Roxanne. "No Respect," *Sports Spectrum* (September-October 2001): 24–25.

Sandrolini, Mike. "The Greatest Story," *Sports Spectrum* (November-December 2000): 24.

_____, assisted by Mike Ostrom. "Spirit of St. Louis," *Sports Spectrum* (November-December 2000): 24–25.

Shacklette, Buddy. "Something Missing," *Sports Spectrum* (December 1999): 20.

_____. "To Protect and Serve," *Sports Spectrum* (December 1999): 18, 21.

Singletary, Mike, with Armen Keteyian. *Calling the Shots* (New York: Contemporary Books, 1986), 30–31, 47.

"Studying the Playbook," *Sports Spectrum* (December 1999): 21.

White, Reggie, with Terry Hill. *Minister of Defense* (Brentwood, Tenn.: Wolgemuth and Hyatt, 1991), 13, 20.

We want to hear from you. Please send your comments about
this book to us in care of the address below. Thank you.

Zonder**kidz**™

Grand Rapids, MI 49530
www.zonderkidz.com